li saennchı di michif

Thomas and the Metis Sash

Written by Bonnie Murray
Illustrated by Sheldon Dawson
Translated by Rita Flamand

Cover and Book Design by: Rhiannon Lynch

Pemmican Publications Inc. gratefully acknowledges the assistance accorded to its publishing program by the Manitoba Arts Council, Canada Arts Council and the Book Publishing Industry Development Program.

Printed and Bound in Canada.

Library and Archives Canada Cataloguing in Publication

Murray, Bonnie 1973-
Li saennchur fleshii di Michif: Thomas and the Metis
Sash / written by Bonnie Murray ; illustrated by Sheldon
Dawson ; translated by Rita Flamand.

Text in English and Michif.
ISBN 1-894717-23-6

1. Metis--Juvenile fiction. 2. Picture books for children. I.
Dawson, Sheldon
II. Flamand, Rita III. Title. IV. Title: Thomas and the Metis Sash.

PS8576.U6745S18 2004   jC813'.6   C2004-906579-3

Pemmican Publications Inc.
"committed to the promotion of Metis culture & heritage."
150 Henry Ave Winnipeg, MB Canada R3B 0J7

This book is dedicated to our
Elders and Teachers...

"Thank you for sharing your knowledge and wisdom. Please continue to pass on the stories, traditions, experiences and history so that we can ensure our culture is sustained for future generations."

-Bonnie Murray

Thomas and his friends were on lunch break one day talking about art class. "I wonder what we'll be making in art class today," said Thomas.

Nicole replied, "I don't know but I bet it will be interesting. We always make neat stuff in that class!"

"Speaking of art class," said Cory, "we better get going to it!" So they put their lunches away and off they went.

Enn jurnnii uta mekwaach li jinnii e-ayaachik Tumaas eekwa sii zamii tashitamuk li klass di-art. "Taannikannaa kekwaay ka ushitaayak dan la klass di-art annuch," itwew Tumaas.

Nikol nashkumeew, "Sipaa, maaka kehchinnaa tamoochikann. Nannaannduk kehkway emiyaashik ki-nitaa ushitaannaann annima li klass!"

"Taapweetakiinn ki kishkishuminn la klass di-art," itwew Kory, "atii ituteetaa sheemaak!" Eekushi eeyishi naashtaachik liu lunnch eekwa ati shipwheetee-wak.

"Good afternoon boys and girls," said Mrs. Roberts. "I hope you had a very good lunch and that you are ready for a "hands-on" art assignment!"

"What does "hands-on" mean?" asked Thomas.

"Well class, what I really mean is FINGERS ON!" said Mrs. Roberts. "Today we are going to learn to finger weave your very own belt! This is what the belt will look like," Mrs. Roberts said as she held up the belt that she had made to show the class.

"Bon zhur lii garsun pi lii fii," itwew madam Ruber. "Ni pahkusheyhiteenn aen bon lunnch ekii ayaayeek eekwa ekiishiitaayeek chi aapachitaayeek tii "maen-iwawa" disiu la art kaa wii ushitaayeek."

"Tannishi maaka annima "lii maen disiu?" eewii itweekî itwew Tumaas.

"Abaen klass, ayii annima eewii itweeyaann LII DWEE! chi aapahchitaahk," itwew madam Ruber.
"Anuch kika nanndo kishkehiteennaann tannishi chi ishi pimitaapeek-inameek ton sancheur-iwaaw! Umishi ton sancheur-iwaw ta ishi naakwann," itwew madam Ruber e-ati upinnak li sancheur kaa kii ushitaat chi waahpah-tahiweet.

"Wow, that's nice, Mrs. Roberts!" said Nicole. "I really like the red and white colors, it reminds me of our Canadian Flag."

"That's right, Nicole," said Mrs. Roberts, "it does resemble the flag! Now you can all come up to the front of the class and pick two colors for your belt and then we'll begin weaving."

All the students then picked their colors. Nicole chose red and white like Mrs. Roberts, Cory chose green and blue, his two favorite colors, and Thomas chose blue and white because it reminded him of the Metis Flag.

"Waahwa, miiyaashinn madam Ruber!" itwew Nikol. "Naashpich ni miiyun-nenn lii kuleur ruuzh pi li blan, sikum ton Kanajien paviyun-innaann e-ishi namaann."

"Si vre, Nikol," itwew madam Ruber, "Sikum li paviyun e-ishi naakuk! Ahaam annavaan kakiyaaw pe ituteek chi pe-kakekinnameek deu kuleur pur tii sancheur-iwaawa eekwa kika maachi pimitaapeekinnikaannaann."

Eekushi tut lii zhaand dikol e-ishi kahkekinnakik liu kuleur. Nikol kahkekinnam li ruuzh pi li blan sikum madam Ruber, Kory kahkekinnam li ver pi li bleu, maawachi emiyunnak, eekwa Tumaas kahkekinnam li bleu pi li blan eekishkishumikut li Paviyun-di-Michif.

"Now that you have chosen the colors for your belt and you have the materials you need I'll explain the steps to finger weaving," said Mrs. Roberts. "Finger weaving takes time so you will weave half of the belt today and finish the other half next class," she explained.

When Thomas and his classmates finished weaving their belts they got to take them home.

"Mom, Dad, look what we made in art class!" Thomas said proudly as he showed his parents his belt.

"Eekushi eekwa ekii kahkekinnameek kel kuleur wii aapachitaayeek pur ton sancheur-iwaw eekwa kakiyaw kitayaannaawaaw kekwaay wii aapachitaay-eek kika kishkinnaamaatinnaawaaw tannishi chi ishi pimitaapeekinikeeyeek," itwew madam Ruber. "Mishtahi li taan aapatann chi pimitaapeekinnikeek. Eekuuchi aaphitaw piko anuch ton sancheur-iwaw kika ushitaannaawaaw eekwa paatimaa la simenn ki vien ki ka kiishitaannaawaaw," wiitamaakuwak.

Eekii kiishi pimitaahpeekinnaakik sii sancheur-iwaw Tumaas avik sii zamii di-kol kii ati kiiwetataahwak sii sancheur-iwawa.

"Mama, papa, chweer kekwaay kaa ushitaayaann dan li klass di-art anuch!" Itwew Tumaas eyishpiichi kichiiteyhitak e-ati wapahatayaat sii peraan son sancheur.

"Wow, Thomas, that's beautiful," said his mom. "I like the colors on it. Is blue your favorite color?" she asked.

"Yes, but I chose these colors because it reminds me of our Metis Flag," Thomas explained.

"That's right, Thomas," his mom said, "it is the same colors as the flag, but do you know what it reminds me of?" she questioned.

"No. What?" Thomas asked.

"Waahwa, miyaashinn, Tumaas," itweyiw umamawa. "Ni miyaapateenn lii kuleur. Li bleu chiin maawachi ki miyehiteenn?" kakweechimiko.

"Wii, maaka nki kakekinnenn onhi lii kuleur akuuz e-kishkishumikuyaann ton paviyun di-Michif-innaann," wiihtamawew Tumaas.

"Taapwee Tumaas," itweeyiw umamawa, "peeyakunn lii kuleur si-kum li paviyun, maaka ki kishkeyhitenn chiin kekwaay e-kishishumikoyaann?" Kahkwechimikoo.

"Noya. Kekwaay?" Kahkwetwew Tumaas.

His mom replied, "The pattern on it reminds me of my Metis Sash!"

"You have a Metis Sash?" Thomas asked.

" Sure, I'll get it so you can see it," his mom said. "Here it is," she said as she held the sash.

"Wow," said Thomas, "it's very colorful and it does have almost the same pattern as my belt! What is it for?" he asked his mom.

Umamawa itweyhiwa, "Li patrun nkishkishumikunn mon Michif-Sancheur-Fleshii!"

"Kitayaann chiin en Michif-Sancheur-Fleshii?" kahkwetweew Tumaas.

"Abaen wii, nka naatenn, chi waahpatamann," itweyhiwa umamawa. "Uuma," itweehiwa e-ati waapahtahikut li sancheur-fleshii.

"Waahwa," itweew Tumaas, "taapwee tut sort di kuleur ishi naakunn kehkaach peyakunn si-kum mon sancheur ishi naakunn! Kekwaay annima uchi?" kahkwechimeew umamawa.

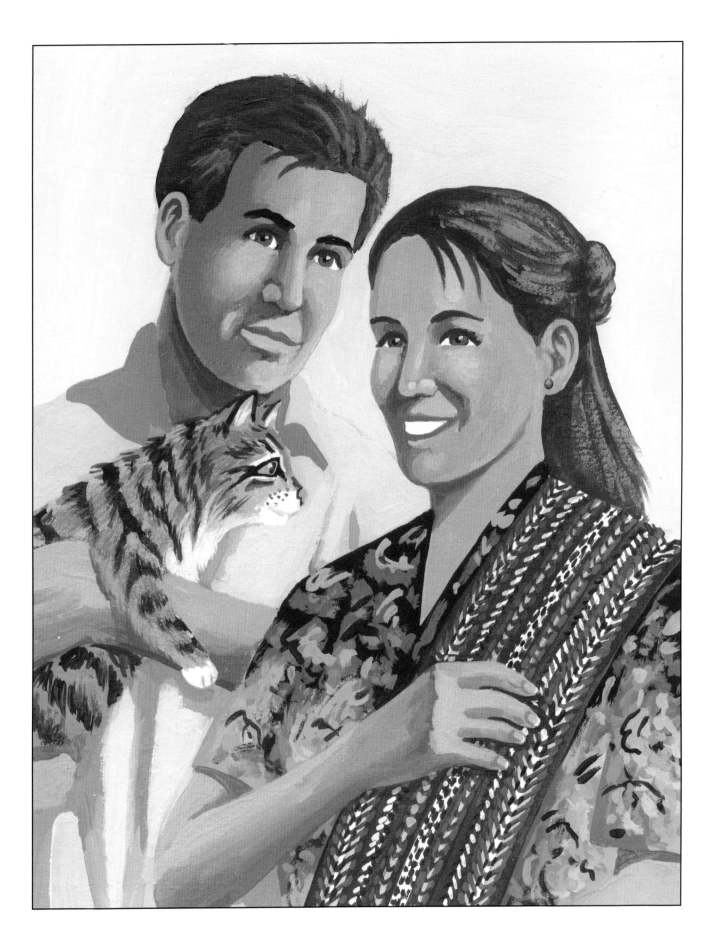

She then explained, "The sash is very special to the Metis people. It can be worn as a scarf, a belt or just tied around the waist and women sometimes wear it over the shoulder. The colors and the pattern on the sash also have a special meaning," his mom said.

Eekushi eeishi wiitamawaat, "Lii Sancheur-Fleshii naashpich lii Michif kichi iteyhitamuk. Si-kum en krimunn taa itaapatann kemaa dan li kor ishi kik-ishkikaatew sikum en sancheur, aashkaw miinna lii faam aagutaawak dan li nipul. Li kuleur pi li patrun dan li sancheur-fleshii miina kichi iteyhitaakunn," itikoo umamawa.

"What is it?" Thomas asked.

"Well," his mom said, "the Metis people feel that the way the sash is woven together with many colors represents how the Metis culture is made up of many different cultural threads like French, Cree, Scottish and Ojibway for example."

"Kekwaay annima?" Kahkwetwew Tumaas.

"Abaen," itweeyiwa umamawa, "lii Michif itweewak annima li sancheur kaa ishi maamawipikaateek avik mishtahi lii kuleur, whapachikaatew taannde pepakaan lii Michif ushitowiniwaw e-uchi payinnihik, si-kum li Fraannse, li Cree, Scottish, pi Ojibwe."

"The Metis people also feel that each color has a special significance. For instance, red is the historical color of the sash, blue and white symbolize the colors of the Metis Flag, green represents fertility, growth and prosperity, and black signifies the dark period in which the Metis people had to endure many hardships."

"*Lii Michif miina itehyitamuk peepeeyak lii kuleur naanndaw itweewano. si-kum takinnee li ruuzh kii pe aapatan pur lii sancheur- fleshii, li bleu pi li blan niipawiishkaatamuk li paviyun-di-Michif , li ver niipawiishaatam pimaatishi-winn, upikiwinn pi kaa miyu pimaachihuk, eekwa li nwer niipawiishkaatam ashpii lii Michif kaa kii pe kakwaatakitaachik.*"

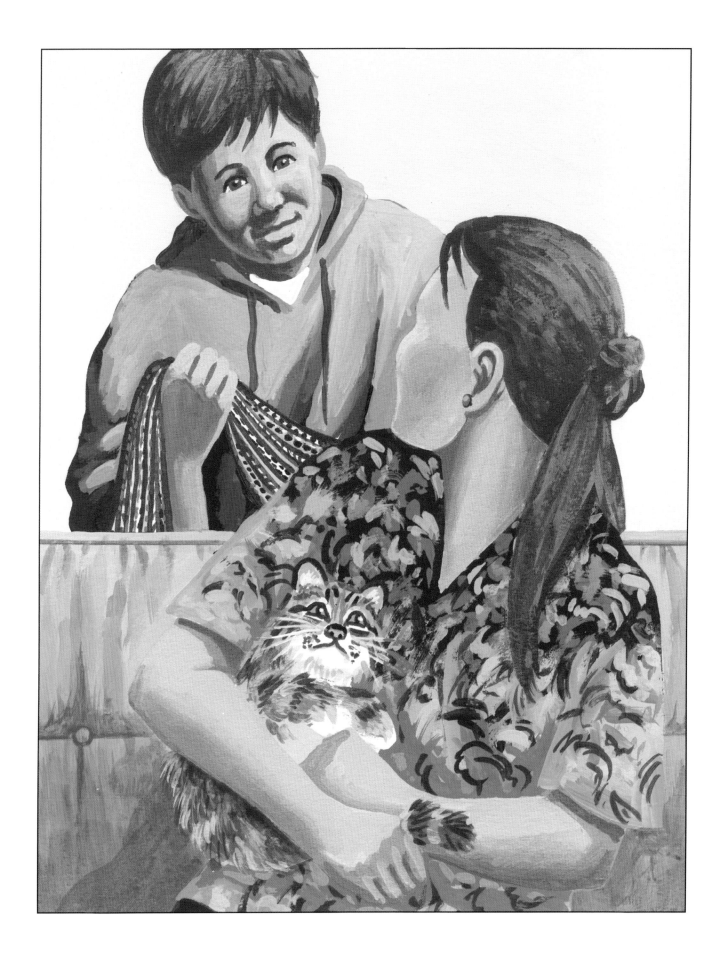

"Wow," said Thomas, "I had no idea the sash was so special. I'm glad you have one, Mom."

"I am too, Thomas," his mom said, "it reminds me to be proud of our unique cultural heritage."

"Mom, can I take your sash to school to show my friends?" Thomas asked.

"Sure," his mom replied.

"Waawha," itwew Tumaas, "Noya ndochi kishkehitenn li sancheur fleshii eishpiichi kichi itehitaakuk. Ni miyehitenn peyak e-ayaayann, mama."

"Niishta miinna, Tumaas," itwehyiwa umamawa, "ni kishkishumikunn chi kichi itehitamaann uma pepakaann kaa ishitowyak."

"Mama, ndaa shipwetataann chiin ton sancheur-fleshii dan li-kol chi waapatayakik mii zamii?" kakwetwew Tumaas.

"Ekushi kwayeshk," Itwehiwa umamawa.

The next day in art class Thomas showed his friends the sash.

"Hey Thomas, what is that?" asked Cory. "It looks like the belts we made."

"You're right, it does," said Thomas. "It's a Metis Sash."

"What is it for?" asked Nicole.

Laandime dan li klass di-art Tumaas waapataayew sii zamii li sancheur.

"Ayii Tumaas, kekwaay annima?" kakwetwew Kory. "Taapishkuuch anihi lii sancheur kaa kii ushitaayak e-ishi naakwak."

"Ki taapwaann, eekushi e-ishi naakwak," itwew Tumaas. "En Michif-Sancheur-Fleshii annima."

"Kekwaay maaka annima uchi?" kakwetweew Nikol.

"It is very special to the Metis people because of the way the colors are blended together like our culture and heritage. The colors have a special meaning too!" said Thomas.

"Really?" asked Cory.

"Yes," said Thomas

He then explained to his friends what the different colors represent and how it reminds his mom to be proud of their Metis heritage.

"Naashpich annima lii Michif kichi iteyhitamuk annihi lii kuleur kaa ishi maa-maweekinikaateki si-kum ki tishitowinninnaann. Eekwa lii kuleur miina kichi iteyhitaakuno!" itweew Tumaas.

"Taapwee?" kakwetwew Kory.

"Wii," itweew Tumaas.

Eekushi e-ishi wiitamawaat sii zamii taannishi lii kuleur pepakaan e-ishi niipawiishtakik eekwa taannishi umamawa e-ishi kishkishumikuyit chi kichi iteyhitak utishitowinniwaaw.

"Wow Thomas, that is something to be proud of," said Nicole.

"Yes, and you were right, Nicole," said Thomas, "we did make something interesting in art class!"

"Hey Thomas," said Cory, "you should tell Mrs. Roberts about your Metis Sash. I bet she will think it's interesting too!"

And so he did.

"Taapwe Tumaas, chi kichi iteyitamik annima," itwew Nikol.

"Wii, eekwa kikii taapwaann, Nikol," itwew Tumaas, "kichi kekway kikii ushitaannaann dan li klass di-art!"

"Ayii Tumaas," itwew Kory, "chi kii aachimushtawat madam Ruber kakiyaaw kekway ton Sancheur-Fleshii uchi. Kechinaa wiishta ta miiyutam!"

Eekushi kaa tuutak.